ICE CREAM MUD

A Fable by Ray Gray

Illustrated by The Clemens Farm Kids

For Nancy

Like Donkey in this story, we all have a path to find in life.
Sometimes we make mistakes and need a kind mate like Horse
to point out our errors and forgive us. The author's mate for
twenty-two years was Nancy Wicklund Gray, who died while
our community art project was in progress.

We dedicate this book to her memory.

About the Book's Creation

The author has told stories to over a million children. He knows that every child responds differently to his stories. The imaginations of eight young artists, ages eight to fourteen, created the illustrations for *Ice Cream Mud*. Though we asked them to draw certain costumes and characteristics for the animals in the story, we did not try to unify the expressions of their imaginations. We have honored each child's vision of the story.

It was a hot, hot summer day.
Under the apple tree stood
Horse, Donkey and Goose.

3

Horse said, "Oh my, it is hot, I need something to cool me."

"Hee haw, hee haw," said Donkey. "I have an idea. How about some ice cream?"

"Yes, yes, yes," said Goose, "that is a fine idea, but where will we get the ice cream?"

4

"Hee haw, hee haw," said Donkey. "I will go to Cow who lives in the barn. She has ice cream and she is willing to share with all."

So they all agreed that Donkey should go to the barn to ask Cow for some of her ice cream.

Now as I said, it was a hot, hot summer day. As Donkey made his way down the road to the barn, the heat rose in waves above the ground. Donkey thought how good the ice cream would taste on this hot, hot summer day.

When Donkey arrived at the barn, he said to Cow, "Hee haw, hee haw, I would like a bucket of vanilla ice cream, a bucket of chocolate ice cream, and a bucket of strawberry ice cream."

Cow scooped down into the cool, creamy vanilla ice cream and carefully filled one bucket. Then she dipped down into the rich, dark chocolate ice cream and filled a second bucket. Finally, she filled a third bucket with the pink ice cream full of juicy, red strawberries.

Donkey thanked Cow for
the ice cream, then balancing
the buckets on a stick,
he started back to his friends
under the apple tree.

The sun was high in the clear sky and it really was a hot, hot summer day. As Donkey made his way back to the apple tree, he thought how good the cold ice cream would taste.

Suddenly he stopped and called out, "Hee haw, hee haw, this ice cream is going to start melting on this hot, hot summer day. Maybe I'd better lick a little of the melted ice cream off the top to keep it all from spoiling."

Who can say whether Donkey thought he was doing the right thing, or whether he just wanted to eat all of the ice cream? First, he opened the cool, creamy vanilla and his big, red tongue skimmed a layer of melted ice cream from the top.

vanilla

11

Then he opened the rich, dark chocolate
and saw that it was melted too,
so he licked deeper into the ice cream.

Finally, he opened the pink ice cream
with juicy, red strawberries
and this time his big, fat tongue
went very deep into the bucket.

Donkey raised his head from the bucket
of strawberry ice cream, licked his whiskers
with his red tongue and looked back to
the vanilla ice cream.
He saw that it had started to melt
again, so he went back and started
a second round of licking more ice
cream from each bucket.

And by the time he started a third round, he could not stop: Around and around he went from vanilla to chocolate to strawberry, vanilla to chocolate to strawberry, vanilla to chocolate to strawberry!

"Hee haw, hee haw," said Donkey as he looked down and saw that almost all of the ice cream was gone, "I've eaten nearly all of the ice cream. Oh, my friends are going to be angry. What can I do?"

16

Donkey looked about for some way to hide the truth.
There at the side of the road he saw a little stream of water.
The bank of the stream was ooey, gooey, brown mud.

Donkey smiled as he thought of a way to trick his friends.
He carried the three buckets over to the stream.

Then Donkey scooped out the little
bit of vanilla ice cream from the
bottom of the bucket, filled the
bucket with mud, and put the vanilla
ice cream back on top. Then he did
the same with the buckets of chocolate
and strawberry ice cream.

"Hee haw, hee haw," said Donkey,
"when my friends find the mud,
I will say it must have been Cow
who put the mud in the ice cream.
She probably ran short of ice cream
on this hot, hot summer day."

So Donkey balanced the buckets
on his stick again and continued on
his way.

Back at the apple tree, it was still a very, very, hot, hot summer day.

Horse closed his eyes and said, "Oh Goose, where is that Donkey? I need some ice cream to cool me."

"Horse, Horse," cried Goose as she looked down the road, "I can see him. Hurry, Horse! Our ice cream is coming!"

Down the road they went to meet Donkey . . . "Clump, clump, clump," sounded Horse's hooves, and . . . "Flap, flap, flap," sounded Goose's wings.

When they came to Donkey, neither one of them greeted him. They just grabbed a bucket and hurried back to the shade of the apple tree.

Horse was first to discover what was in the bucket. He dipped down into what he thought was cool, creamy vanilla ice cream.

"Ah, ah, ah, blaaah!" cried out Horse as he spit out the ice cream mud.

Then Goose dipped down into what she thought was rich, dark chocolate ice cream.

"Nah, nah, nah, naaah!" cried out Goose as she spit out the ice cream mud.

Angrily Goose called to Donkey who was slowly walking up the road toward the apple tree. "You did this Donkey; you put mud in our ice cream!"

"Hee haw, hee haw," said Donkey with his head down. "It wasn't me, it must have been Cow. She probably ran short of ice cream on this hot, hot summer day."

Donkey raised his head to see if his friends believed his lie.

"You, You, YOU, Donkey!" cried Goose, "You put the mud in the buckets. You ate our ice cream. I can see it all over your whiskers — vanilla, chocolate and strawberry! You will be punished for this!"

"No, Goose," said Horse calmly, "I don't think we need to punish Donkey. Look at his belly; see how full of ice cream it is. And look at his face; see how bad he feels about telling a lie to his friends. I don't think he will ever be tempted to eat so much ice cream again; but more importantly, he will never be tempted to tell another lie like this one about ice cream mud!"

As an illustrator and designer — and a mom — I found Ray's wish to have neighborhood children illustrate his story a happy choice. I watched the children as they listened to Ray's telling of *Ice Cream Mud* at our first meeting, and could see his expressive acting and voices enhanced the emotion of the tale for the kids. It made it easy to prompt them into imagining costumes and characteristics for the animal actors in his story, and helped bring about the variety of facial expressions they eventually drew in their pictures.

I found the kids' artwork to be charming complements to this barnyard tale. I hope it inspires more stories and more drawings from The Clemens Farm Kids as they grow, and from other children as they read this and imagine what they too can create in story and pictures.

— *Pat Achilles*

Ray Gray and all of the young artists live on land that once was part
of the Clemens Family Farm.
The artists are listed here alphabetically by last name:

Olivia Barrett
Sofie Fitzmartin
Ainsley Massey
Madelynn Massey

Grant Massey
J T Massey
Marco Pocai
Sofia Pocai

Made in the USA
Lexington, KY
12 November 2019